A promise kept . . . Jim and Cilly Littlewood
K. L.

Text and illustrations copyright © Karin Littlewood 2010
The right of Karin Littlewood to be identified as the author and illustrator of this work
has been asserted by her in accordance with the Copyright, Designs and Patents Act,
1988 (United Kingdom).

First published in Great Britain in 2010 by Gullane Children's Books

This edition published in Great Britain in 2016 by
Otter-Barry Books
Little Orchard, Burley Gate, Herefordshire, HR1 3QS

A catalogue record for this book is available from the British Library.

ISBN 978-1-91095-953-4

Illustrated with watercolour, gouache and pencil

Printed in China

1 3 5 7 9 8 6 4 2

IMMI

IMMI

Karin Littlewood

Otter-Barry BOOKS

Oh, it was cold.
The icy wind blew, and the snow fell and fell.
Immi looked around her, but all she could see
was a frozen, white world.

Immi broke a hole through the ice and fished for her supper.
"Just one more," she thought, "in case anyone comes round. . ."
which they hardly ever did.

But, instead of a fish, at the end of the line
she found a little wooden bird.

It was so beautiful!
She'd never seen
such colours before.

And she tied it to her necklace,
next to a small white bear.

The next day Immi fished a red flower.

Then an
orange starfish . . .

a green leaf . . .

a purple feather . . .

and soon her igloo was the
brightest thing in the land!

It could be seen for miles around.
And, before long, visitors came
from far and wide to
look and to wonder.

They always stayed for supper,
and they filled those long, dark nights
with stories of faraway lands.

And Immi's world seemed a brighter
and more colourful place.

Then one day the ice began to melt.
It was time for her to leave.

But just as Immi was about to go,
she stopped and put her hand
to her necklace. She took the
small bear and gently
dropped it into the water.

Then she turned and left.

Far away, a little boy walks across a beach,
holding the brightest thing he can find.
He throws it into the waves and wonders,
as he always does, where it will go.

But this time something catches
his eye, shining in the sand.

It is a beautiful, small white bear.

He picks it up and holds it.
Then he hangs it around his neck,
where a little wooden bird
had once hung.

KARIN LITTLEWOOD has illustrated over 40 children's books,
and her work has been nominated three times for the Kate Greenaway Medal.
She regularly gives illustration workshops at festivals, schools, libraries and bookshops
across the UK. Her books include *The Colour of Home*, with Mary Hoffman,
which was chosen as one of the top 50 titles celebrating cultural diversity,
Moonshadow, with Gillian Lobel, *When Dad Was Away*, with Liz Weir,
and *Star Girl*, which she wrote and illustrated.
Karin lives in north London.